JOHN WORSLEY

The illustrations by John Worsley in the *Golden Classics* series, have greatly added to the impact and charm of these dramatic stories. Now well-established as a portrait painter and marine artist, John Worsley was in the Royal Navy during the war. Taken prisoner, he and a fellow officer constructed an astonishingly life-like dummy to help in their escape plan. After the war he was appointed adviser to the makers of the famous war film, *Albert RN,* which tells the true story of this remarkable feat.

Daniel Defoe's
ROBINSON CRUSOE

Retold by Jane Carruth

 GOLDEN PRESS · NEW YORK
Western Publishing Company, Inc.
Racine, Wisconsin

The call of the sea

I WAS BORN in the year 1632, in the city of York, of a good family. I was the third son of the family and had no inclination to follow a special trade. Instead, from an early age, I became intent on seeing the world.

As I grew older, nothing would satisfy me but to go to sea. My father earnestly begged me to give up this intention, but I continued to be obstinately deaf to all his arguments which, on reflection, were both logical and sensible. So it was, in the September of 1651, when I was but eighteen years old, that I boarded a ship at Hull without telling him or my mother.

My first voyage was by no means a success. We were beset perpetually by storms and I discovered early that I had a very weak stomach. The voyage ended with the ship sinking beneath us in a terrible storm, and we had to be taken off our ship by boat. When I saw her sink, within fifteen short minutes, I understood then, for the first time, what was meant by a ship foundering in the sea.

If I had had any sense I would have gone back home, but this I could not bring myself to do, lest my father should point out the accuracy of his earlier warnings. Instead, I began to look out for another ship.

Thus it was that over the next few years I made voyage after voyage. The only one which I may call successful in all my adventuring was when I joined a band of honest traders on a voyage to Guinea. With help and guidance from a truly good

man I set up as a trader in that place and for a time led a comfortable and quite prosperous life. But when my partner died, I made up my mind to return to London with money in my pocket. Once again, there was an opportunity to go home to York, but still I could not face it. Instead, after a short time, I set sail for Guinea once more, but this voyage proved to be the unhappiest ever made by man. As our ship was making her course towards the Canary Islands, we were surprised in the gray of the morning by a Turkish rover who chased us with all the sail she could make.

We, in our turn, put up as much canvas as our masts could take to get away, but the pirate ship still gained on us. It was clear she would catch up with us in a few hours so we prepared to fight. Our ship had twelve guns but the rover had eighteen.

About three in the afternoon she came up alongside, and we immediately fired eight of our guns at her, which made her sheer off again. But straight away she prepared to attack again, this time with more success. Sixty of the pirates

clambered on our decks and began cutting and hacking the sails and rigging. We fought them with small shot, half pikes and anything else we could lay our hands on. But when three of our men were killed and eight wounded, we were obliged to yield.

The remainder of us were taken as prisoners and landed at Sallee, a port belonging to the Moors. Most of our men were almost immediately carried up country to the Emperor's court. But I was kept by the captain of the pirate ship as his prize, and made his personal slave.

Slavery and escape

MY NEW master took me home to his house, and I hoped repeatedly that he would take me with him when next he went to sea. I believed that it would be his fate to be captured by a Spanish or Portuguese man-of-war which of course would mean that I would be given my liberty.

But this hope soon began to fade, for when he went to sea he left me on shore to look after his garden and do the common drudgery of slaves about his house. When he returned from each trip, he ordered me to live in the cabin and look after the ship.

For two years or more I puzzled as to how I could best make my escape. But there was no one of my own kind to whom I could look for any assistance.

Then, one day, it happened that when I was out fishing with my master, accompanied also by one of his kinsmen, a fog rose so thickly that we lost sight of the shore. We rowed this way and that all day and half the night. When morning came, we found we had pulled out to sea instead of pulling in for shore.

We reached the shore safely at length, but not without a great deal of hard work and some danger. Learning from this misadventure, my master resolved to take more care when he went out fishing, saying that he would not fish again without a compass and some provisions. Then he ordered his carpenter to build an extra cabin on the long-boat of our English ship — the very same that he had captured — and into this he put a table, chairs and some lockers so that he might stock up with bottles of wine, bread, rice and coffee.

I accompanied my master frequently on his fishing trips for I was extremely clever at catching fish. Now, it happened one day

that he had arranged to go out in this boat with two or three Moors — friends of his — and we were told to take on board a larger store of provisions than usual.

I got all the things ready as he had directed and by the next morning the boat was washed clean and the pennants were flying.

As I was waiting, my master appeared. "You are to take the boat out yourself," he said to me. "My friends are unable to come. But see to it that you bring back a good quantity of fish."

On hearing this, it seemed to me that my chance had come at last to escape. After he had gone back to the house, my first action was to persuade the Moor, who was to come with me, to bring aboard a supply of rusks or biscuits and three jars of water, telling him we must not use our master's provisions. I told him also that we might need powder and shot on board in case we had the chance to shoot some water fowl, all of which he accepted without question.

When the boat was loaded, we set sail. I should have mentioned that besides the Moor, a young slave boy, called Xury, was also aboard. When we were some little way out, we began to fish. What fish I caught on my hook I immediately let go without

the Moor's knowledge, and after awhile I said to him, "This will not do. Our master is expecting us to return with a big catch. We will have to try farther out."

The Moor agreed and we sailed away from the shore. When we were a mile or so out, I crept up behind the Moor and, taking him by surprise, I pushed him overboard into the sea. He swam like a fish, straight after our boat, so I shouted to him, "Turn around and swim to the shore and I will do you no harm. But if you come

near the boat, I'll shoot your head off!"

He did as I said and swam for the shore. Immediately I turned to the boy. "If you will be faithful to me," I said, "I'll make you a great man. If not, I must throw you into the sea after him."

The boy smiled with such trust and swore to be faithful to me that I spared his life and kept him on board with me.

Under cover of darkness, I changed my course and began to steer directly south and east, all the while keeping within sight of the shore. The strong fresh wind and smooth quiet sea seemed to favor me and we made fair progress through the water. By the next day I was sure we would be at least one hundred and fifty miles away from Sallee.

After making excellent progress for five days, I decided to try and land. We came to anchor in the mouth of a little river. We neither saw, nor wished to see, any people. My chief need and desire was for fresh water.

We sailed into the creek in the evening and I resolved to swim ashore as soon as dusk had fallen. But no sooner was it dark, than we heard such horrifying noises of wild creatures barking, roaring and howling, that Xury, who until then had been in good spirits, was ready to die of fear.

"Master no go!" he begged. "In daylight we give them the shoot gun and then they run!"

Laughing a little at his peculiar English, I agreed. We dropped our anchor and prepared to stay all night in the creek. I did not sleep, however, and some time later we saw vast great creatures of many sorts come down to the seashore and run into the water, wallowing and washing themselves. They made the most hideous howling that I had ever heard.

Xury was dreadfully frightened and so was I when I saw one of these mighty creatures come swimming towards our boat. It came so close that I took up my gun and fired at it. Happily it immediately turned about and swam back towards the land.

In the morning, however, we had to go ashore as we were now completely out of water. We took the boat as near as possible to the shore and then waded to the land, each carrying nothing but two jars for water. A little higher up the creek we found fresh water, so we filled our jars and prepared to return to our boat, relieved not to have been seen by the wild creatures who inhabited that place.

Soon afterwards, however, when we were once again obliged to land for fresh water, Xury called softly, "Look, master! A dreadful monster lies on the side of that hillock, fast sleep!"

The 'great monster' was no less than a huge, terrible lion. Raising my gun, I took the best aim I could at him. My shot wounded him in the leg so that he awoke with a blood-chilling roar. My next shot was more accurate and I saw him drop to the ground. I would have left him where he lay if I had not thought that one day his skin might be of some value to me. So, with Xury's assistance, I skinned that monstrous beast, and the sun dried the hide within two days' time. I may add that it served me well as something soft to lie upon.

Wrecked on a desert island

WE MADE our way southwards for ten or twelve days, living sparingly on our provisions. My aim was to reach the River Gambia or Senegal where I hoped to meet with some European ship.

When we were once again desperately in need of fresh water, we sailed close to land and there saw people standing upon the shore looking at us. They were black-skinned and naked but they had no weapons in their hands. I kept the boat at a distance but made signs to them that we were in need of food, and presently two of them went away and came back in less than half-an-hour with pieces of dried fish and some corn. They put these on the shore and then stood some way off until we had fetched them on board.

Back on our boat we looked again towards the shore, and there were two mighty creatures, one chasing the other, racing down the mountains towards the sea. The natives were terrified and scattered in all directions. But, as one of the creatures came near to the shore, I fired and shot him in the head. He fell immediately.

It is impossible to express the astonishment of these poor natives at the noise of my gun. But when they saw that one of the creatures that had killed so many of their women was now dead, they began dancing and singing for joy.

I waded ashore again and on examination found that I had shot a fine spotted leopard. I was more than happy to accept the skin which the natives offered as my prize for shooting it.

Soon we set sail again, this time with fresh water and dried meat and corn. And there that voyage ended as within a short time we were spotted by a Portuguese ship, and taken aboard.

The captain was a most generous gentleman and took us all the way to Brazil, refusing payment of any kind. Indeed, not only would he take no money

from me whatsoever, he even gave me twenty ducats for the leopard skin. On landing, he made an offer for Xury and on finding the boy was willing to go with him I agreed. But it was with a heavy heart that I watched the young lad who had helped me to freedom leave the ship with his new master.

All would have been well with me if I had once again decided to settle, for I acquired a plantation in Brazil and was on the way to prospering. As it was, I had lived but four short years on it, when a company of merchants and planters, all friends of mine, asked me to take their ship to the coast of Guinea where I would do some trading for them.

I could no more resist this proposition than I had been able to resist my first chance to go to sea, and so I accepted.

Thus it was that on the 1st September 1659, I went on board once more. Our ship was about one hundred and twenty tons with six guns and fourteen men besides the master, his boy and myself. On the day that I boarded her we set sail for the African coast.

To begin with we had very good weather.

Then, after some weeks at sea, a violent hurricane took us all by surprise. It blew in such a dreadful manner that for twelve days we could do nothing but let it take us where it would.

After those terrible twelve days the weather improved, and as our ship was in need of attention we changed our course and headed northwest trying to reach some English islands. But scarcely had we done so than a second storm came upon us carrying us due west and then quite out of the way of all human commerce.

We had lost two men and the boy in the previous storm and those left on board were greatly afraid. The wind continued to blow. Then, early one morning, a man in the bows cried out, "Land!" No sooner had we run out of the cabin to look for ourselves than the ship struck a sandbank and, in a moment, the sea began breaking over her in such a manner that we expected we should all perish forthwith.

We had had a boat at our stern just before the storm, but she was long since lost at sea. We had another boat on board, but how were we to get her off into the water?

Finally the mate, with the help of the rest of the men, got her slung over the ship's side, and we all climbed into her, committing ourselves to God's mercy and the wild sea.

We pulled as well as we could towards land, but after we had rowed about a mile or so a raging wave, as high as a mountain, came rolling over us. In one small second, it upset the boat and cast us all separately into the swirling sea.

Nothing can describe my thoughts as I sank into that savage water, for though I was a strong swimmer, I had no hope of saving myself from the force of the waves. My whole concentration was taken up in keeping my head above water, at least whenever possible, until a wave, larger than the others, carried me up on to the shore. Having spent itself, it left me on dry land, but half-dead with all the water I had swallowed.

Before the next giant wave came roaring over me, I kept a light hold on a piece of rock. Then, in between waves, and using all the strength I had left, I was finally able to clamber up the cliffs of the shore and cast myself down on the grass. At last I was free from danger and out of reach of the merciless water.

Safe on shore, I began to look about me, and to thank God that my life was saved. As I recovered somewhat I tried to ascertain what place I was in. My clothes were soaking, I had no food, and only a knife with which to defend myself. When darkness fell, a mood of deep despair took hold of me, but I resolved to find a thick bushy tree in which I might spend the night. This I did almost immediately and having cut a short stick, like a truncheon, to aid my defense, I took up my lodging. The events of the day soon overtook me and I fell fast asleep.

My first few weeks

WHEN I AWOKE it was broad daylight. The weather was clear, and the storm had abated, so that now the sea was calm. To my great surprise our ship had been lifted off the sandbank and was now driven up almost as far as the rock which had been, in part, my savior.

By the afternoon, the tide had ebbed so far out that I could come within a quarter of a mile of the ship. It was then that I could not hold my grief back, for if we had kept on board we would all have been safe. I resolved to get to the ship, so I pulled off my clothes, for the weather was extremely hot, and took to the water. When I came to the ship, I swam round her twice, and the second time I spied a small piece of rope. I caught hold of it and was able to climb into the forecastle. Here I found that though she had shipped a great deal of water which was lying in the hold, all her quarter was free.

I found that all the ship's provisions were dry and untouched by water, so I took a handful of biscuits which I ate as I went about. There were so many things on the ship that would be useful to me that I saw I must make a raft to take them off to the island. I set to, roping large spars of wood together.

When my raft was strong enough, I loaded her up with provisions — bread, rice, cheese and goat's meat, and some European corn — which had been laid by for some fowls, now all killed and eaten.

As for clothes, I found enough to fit me out for a number of years! Then, after a long search, I came upon the carpenter's chest, which at this time was more valuable to me than a ship-load of gold.

When my raft was pretty well loaded, I put to sea, hoping to find some creek or river which I might make use of as a port in order to land with my cargo.

Presently, as I imagined, there appeared before me a little opening of the land and I found a strong current of the tide flowing into it, so I guided my raft as well as I could, to keep it in the middle of the stream. There I was forced to wait until the tide was at its highest, at which time I thrust her upon a flat piece of ground and moored her. After the water had ebbed away, my raft was high and dry and all my cargo was safe on shore!

My next job, it seemed to me, was to view the country and look for a place to settle. I took out one of the fowling-pieces, and one of the pistols, and a horn of powder, and thus armed I climbed a hill that I had seen not a mile from my cove.

Imagine my feelings when I found that I was on a barren island, completely uninhabited except for wild beasts, of which, however, I saw none. I saw plenty of strange-looking fowls, and one great bird which I shot; it looked like a hawk but had no talons or claws and its flesh was not fit to eat.

That night, I barricaded myself around with chests and boards for protection and, in the morning, went on board the ship as before, resolved to bring back bags of nails and spikes and screws, and indeed, anything else that would be useful to me on my island.

After thirteen days on my desert island, I had made eleven journeys to the ship and had all but stripped her bare. I used her sails to make a tent for myself, and to wrap up some of my perishable goods in canvas.

It was just as well I had worked so diligently for, on the fourteenth day, the wind began to blow very hard and the next morning when I looked out to sea, no ship was to be seen!

Although thoughts of escape and rescue were never far from my thoughts, I clearly had to find a proper place to live in the meantime. I searched all over the island until I came across a little plain on the side of a rising hill, whose front was as steep as the side of a house, so that nothing could come down upon me from the top. On the other side was a hollow place, which I saw I could make into a more substantial cave. On the flat of the green, I made up my mind to pitch my tent. But before doing so, I drove two rows of strong stakes into the ground in a half-circle, so that they

stood very firm. Then I strengthened my fence with pieces of cable, and made an entrance, not by a door, but by a short ladder which went over the top of the fence and could be lifted over after me.

With infinite labor I carried all my riches into my fortress. I made a large tent, to shield me from the rains, and covered it with tarpaulin I had salvaged.

It cost me a great deal of hard work and many days before I was able to dig my way into the rocky hillside and make myself a cave, just behind my tent. But when it was finished, it served as the cellar to my new house. It was with some satisfaction that I finally sat back on my heels to take stock of my work.

As a rest from my labors, I occasionally went out with my gun. I was pleased to find goats on the island, and one day I killed a she-goat, which had a little kid at her side. I took the kid in my arms and carried it back to my fortress, hoping to make it tame. It would not eat, however, and I was forced to kill it, too.

After a few weeks on my desert island, it came to me that I would lose my reckoning of time. So, to prevent this, on a large post I carved out the words: *I came on shore here on the 30th September 1659.* Then I made a crude calendar with knife notches and each day I saw to it that I kept this up to date.

Counting my blessings

ALTHOUGH I have not yet mentioned it, I was not entirely lacking in company for, on one of my voyages to the ship, I had found the ship's two cats and the captain's dog. These three animals became my sole companions and the dog a loyal friend and ally in my hunting trips.

In addition, I had managed to salvage three Bibles in good condition, and some pens, ink and paper. From that day I began my Journal which I meant to keep most faithfully.

Despite the time it took to enter all the events which overtook me on the island, I worked hard on making myself the necessities that would make my life more bearable. I made a table and chair. And I made a number of large wicker baskets, having at one time learned the art of basket-weaving.

I constructed large shelves in my cellar on which I stored everything neatly away, and knocked pieces into the wall of the rock so I could hang up my guns. Now I had everything ready to hand and this gave me great pleasure, although I was frequently overcome by moods of deep depression as I thought of the hopelessness of my plight.

It grew dark by seven each evening and having no wax to make candles, I saved the tallow whenever I killed a goat. I placed it in a little dish made of clay and baked it in the sun. Then I added a wick of some oakum. Thus I made my first lamp and at least it gave me some light, though admittedly not so good as that of a candle.

In the midst of all my rummaging through the goods I had salvaged, I found a small bag filled with corn. I shook the husks out on one side of my fortress under the rock. Shortly afterwards the great rains came and, to my astonishment, sometime later I saw a few green stalks shooting out of the ground. This was to be the beginning of my crop-growing.

After some nine months on my island, I had made a detailed survey of it, and was surprised to find it yielded many different fruits. In particular, I found large melons which lay on the ground, and clusters of grapes, which grew on vines spread over the trees. I took the grapes back to my home and dried them in the sun, thinking that dried grapes or raisins would be most wholesome and agreeable to eat when the

fresh grape season was over. In addition I found limes and lemons and I collected and stored all these fruits for future sustenance, for who knew how long I was to find myself marooned here?

The rains began in earnest about the middle of August eleven months after my arrival on the island. So violent were they that I could not stir out of my cave for several days, and I was greatly surprised at the increase of my family during this time. I had been concerned when one of my cats ran away from me and did not return, but to my astonishment, she came home about the end of August with three kittens. The young cats were the same kind of breed as their mother, and as both the ship's cats

were female, I thought it strange. But from these three kittens I afterwards came to be so pestered with cats that I was forced to drive them away from my house as soon as I saw them.

When the rains stopped at last, I made another trip round the island and came back with yet more additions to the family. My dog had seized a young kid by the leg and so I carried it home. I was determined to try to rear goats again.

I caught a young parrot as well, after much trouble, and so I took this home, too. I set about teaching him to talk, but it was some years before he said anything.

When he did, however, he called me by my name in a most familiar fashion, which never failed to amuse me.

As I continued to explore my island, it gradually came to me that it was possible for me to be more happy in this forsaken place than I had imagined. And, at last, I was able to give thanks to God for bringing me to this deserted place.

A boat and a new outfit

WITH THE passing of the years, I found a great deal to employ me. I had long desired to make some large earthenware vessels to hold my dry corn. I tried many times and many ways to do this but none was successful, so at last I set myself to study how I might make use of my fire, using it perhaps to burn some pots. I had little notion of a kiln, such as the potters use, or the principles of glazing pots. But I placed three large pans and two or three of my fashioned clay pots in a pile, one upon the other. I heaped firewood all around, with a large amount of embers under them. Then I sat back and observed as the pots grew red-hot inside. Amazingly they did not crack. When I saw them glow clear red, I left them to stand in the heat for about five or six hours, watching over my fire so that it never grew too hot. In the morning, when they had grown quite cold, I found I had three very good pans and two earthen pots burnt hard.

After this experiment, I went on to make every kind of earthenware for my needs.

In spite of my relative peace and happiness all the while I was busy, my thoughts were occupied with the desire to find some means of escape. I began wondering if I could make myself a canoe, even though I had only crude, elementary tools, out of the trunk of some great tree.

I was twenty days hacking and hewing at the cedar tree that seemed right for my purpose. Then it cost me near three months more to clear the inside, and scrape it out so as to make an exact boat of

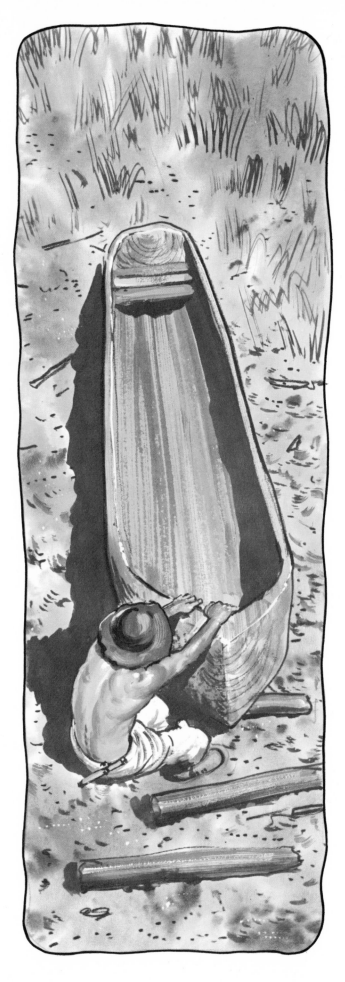

it. But when the work was finished, I was extremely delighted with the look of my canoe.

Imagine my grief when I found it was too heavy for me to get to the water, and after many futile attempts I had to confess to myself that the entire enterprise had been a dismal failure.

From the reckoning of my journal and calendar I had now been on the island some four years. My clothes had begun to decay, and the thick watch-coats that had once belonged to the seamen were really too hot to wear. The weather on my island was so violently hot that in truth there was little need of clothes, yet I could not bring myself to go naked. In the same way, I would always wear a cap or a hat to shield me from the heat of the sun.

Eventually my lack of clothes forced me to set to work tailoring, or perhaps botching would be a better word, for I made most piteous work of it. After much trial and error and loss of temper, however, I managed to make two or three vests, of a kind, which I hoped would serve me a long while.

As I mentioned, I always saved the skins of the creatures I had killed, and I had hung them up, stretched out with sticks, in the sun. The first thing I made from these was a great hat for my head, with the hair on the outside, to keep the rain off me. This was so successful that I began making myself a suit of clothes wholly out of goatskin. I made a vest, and a pair of breeches open at the knees. Both were loose, so as to keep me cool.

After this, I spent a great deal of time and pains in making an umbrella. I was, indeed, in very great need of one, and had a mind to make one like those I had seen in the Brazils, where they are very useful as protection against the great heat. However, my attempts were not successful and I spoiled two or three before I had made one that answered to my purpose. It was covered with skins, the hair upwards, so that the rain would shoot off it, and kept off the sun so well that I could walk out in the hottest of the weather. When I had no need of it, I could close it and carry it under my arm.

A narrow escape

AFTER SOME years on my island with no sign of rescue, I again began to think about the best way to escape. In spite of my last failure I could think only of making another canoe. This time however, I resolved not to attempt a great heavy boat, but a small light one which would be easy to move. I decided too, to make it close to the creek, so the transport would be less of a problem. I began my labors and finally, after much toil, my canoe was finished. Then I dug a canal from it, six feet wide and four feet deep, down to the creek. All that was left was to steer it down the canal to the water.

The smallness of my boat, however, put an end to my dream of escaping from the island. But I fitted it up with a little mast, and made a sail out of some of the pieces of the ship's sail, which I had still in store. I cut a long hollow place in the inside of the boat, where I could lay my gun, and made a flap to hang down over it to keep it dry.

Then I fixed my umbrella at the stern so that it stood over my head, and shielded me from the heat of the sun. Every now and then, I would go for a sail along the coastline, but I never ventured far out to sea.

At last, however, on the sixth of November, in the sixth year of my stay, I set out on a much longer voyage, and one I had not so far undertaken. That was to sail around the east side of the island.

There I made a kind of anchor with a piece of broken grappling which I had taken from the ship, and, having secured the boat, I took my gun and went on shore. There was lots of wild life at this end of the island and I was able to stock up well with provisions. Indeed I was having so much success I resolved to stay away from home for two days. On the third day I loaded up my little boat, pushed off and jumped in, ready to sail back to my home. It was then that disaster struck for I was not even my boat's length from the shore when I found myself in a great depth of water caught up in a violent current.

I saw the danger of being swept out to sea in an instant but I was quite powerless to prevent it. In fact, I was ready to give myself up for lost.

It is impossible to describe my distress when I found myself being carried away aimlessly from my island. Towards noon, a breeze of wind began blowing in my face, and I labored harder than ever to turn the boat landwards.

I set my mast and sail and as it began to stretch, I saw by the clearness of the water that some change in the current was near. The wind suddenly began to freshen and all at once to my joyous, relief, I found myself in a strong eddy, which flowed back again to shore.

After five hours, I found myself in smooth water again and after what seemed like an eternity, I was able to pull my boat up on shore. Straight away I fell on my knees and gave thanks to God for my deliverance.

I left the canoe in an inlet where I had come ashore and, not wanting to weigh myself down, I took nothing out of her but my gun and my umbrella. I managed to assess my position on the island and set off to my home. I reached my fortress in the evening and there was my Poll calling,

"Robin, Robin, Robin Crusoe! Poor Robinson Crusoe! Where are you? Where are you? Where have you been?"

Comforted by his welcome, I called him to me, and he came and sat upon my thumb, as he always did, and continued to talk nonsense to me. I soon felt better.

This adventure put an end to my voyages, and I remained at home, perfecting my earthenware and improving my wicker-baskets, straying away only to hunt and check all was well on my island.

In the eleventh year of my residence, and with my ammunition growing low, I set myself to study how best I could trap and snare the goats. At length I was able to set three traps, quite new in design to me at least, and the next morning was more

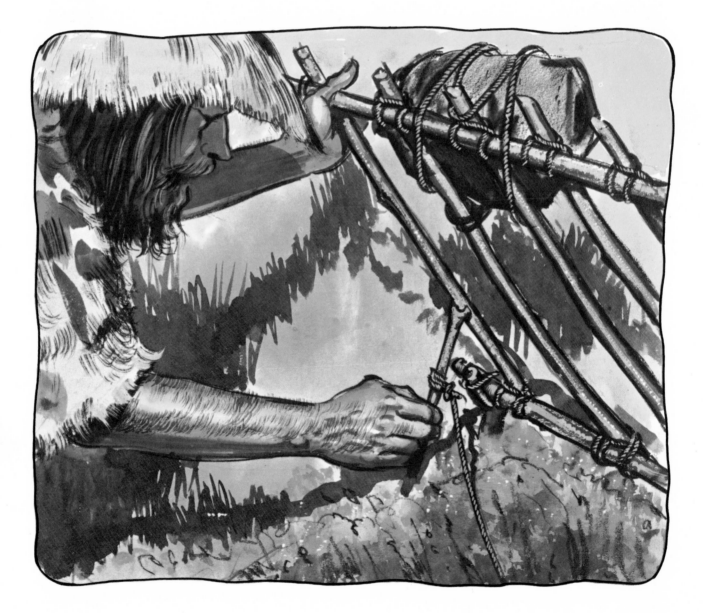

than delighted to find I had caught a large old he-goat in one and in another, three kids — one male and two females.

The old one was so fierce that I dared not go into the pit to him, so I left the trap door open for him and he ran away. One by one, I tied the three kids together with strings, and then with some difficulty, I led them all home.

I kept them tied near my fortress and it was a good while before they would feed. I used to throw sweet-corn to them and finally they were tempted by it, and soon they began to grow tame. Then it occurred to me that I must keep them from the wild goats, or they would soon run wild again. With this in mind, I began enclosing a piece of ground with fencing. It was a great labor without proper tools, and my enclosure took me close on three months to complete. By that time my goats were following me up and down, bleating for corn, which they ate out of my hand.

In two years, I had forty-three goats and kids, besides the ones I had to kill for food. I was perpetually enclosing more pieces of ground to feed them in, with little pens to drive them into, and gates so I could take them from one piece of ground to another. As a goat farmer it seemed I was a success!

The print of a man's foot

IT WOULD HAVE made you smile to have seen me and my little family sit down to dinner. Like a king, I dined alone, attended by servants! Poll, as if he had been my favorite, was the only person permitted to talk to me. My dog, who was now old and failing, sat always at my right hand; and the two cats, one on one side of the table and one on the other, sat expecting now and then a tidbit from my hand, as a mark of special favor.

Having long since retrieved my boat, I would wander down to it sometimes after dinner. It happened, one day in the afternoon, going on such a trip, that I saw, to my great surprise and horror, the print of a man's naked foot in the sand! I stood like one thunderstruck, or as if I had seen

That night I slept not at all. But in the morning I decided that my resolution to stay at my fortress would be of no benefit, so taking courage, I began to steal abroad. However, I went about with such fear in my heart that I could scarcely attend to milking my goats.

I had lived fifteen years upon my island without seeing the least shadow or figure of any people. All I could imagine was that savages were now coming from the mainland to plunder the rich fertile valley. I started at once to strengthen my wall, and take all the measures human prudence would suggest for my own preservation.

Next I set about preserving my herds of goats, and spent some time searching out the most remote parts of the island. In the middle of some thick woods, I found a clear piece of land, and after fencing it in, I drove my goats there. The dread and terror of falling into the hands of savages and cannibals affected my spirits so deeply that I could scarcely apply myself to prayer and my sleep was always disturbed and troubled.

One morning when I came down to the shore from the southwest, I was completely confounded and amazed for there on the sand were skulls and bones that I knew belonged to human bodies. When I overcame some of my horror I saw where a fire had been made and around it a circular mound on which I supposed the savages had feasted on their fellow creatures.

I could not bear to stay in that place any longer, and once more I sought sanctity in my castle. Calmer then, I began to think on my discovery. Clearly, the cannibals did not come to my island to take away its spoils, but only to celebrate certain kinds of feasting.

Time, however, and the satisfaction I had that I was in no danger of being found by these cannibals, began to give me a certain peace of mind. I even began to contemplate how best I could overcome them should they visit the island again. All of my fancies and schemes came to nothing, however, for no savages came near me for a great while.

an apparition. I listened, I looked round me, but I could hear nothing, nor see anything. I went up and down the shore and then came back to the spot, hoping that perhaps after all I had only imagined it. But there it was, the print of a foot — toes, heel and every part of a foot.

Terrified to the last degree, looking behind me at every two or three steps, and fancying every stump of tree to be a man, I went home to my fortress. Never did a frightened hare run to its lair or a fox to its earth, with more terror of mind than I to my castle.

The rescue

ABOUT A YEAR and a half after these events, when I had all but forgotten them, I was surprised one morning to see no less than five canoes all on shore together on my side of the island. The people who must have travelled in them had obviously already come ashore and were nowhere to be seen. Having waited very still for a good while, listening to hear if they made any noise, I took up my guns and climbed to the top of the hill. I then observed, by the help of my perspective glass, that they were no less than thirty in number; and that they had a fire kindled. This they were dancing around, waving their arms in barbarous gestures.

As I watched, two miserable wretches were dragged to the scene. One was immediately knocked to the ground with a club, and to my intense revulsion, two of the savages began to cut him up. The other victim, left standing by himself for a moment, started to run away from them, moving with incredible swiftness in my direction.

I was dreadfully frightened, I must confess, when I saw him approaching. Then I saw that he was being pursued by only two of the savages and it occurred to me that I was called by Providence to save him.

With my guns at the ready I ran down the hill, and managed to place myself between the pursuers and the pursued. Shouting and beckoning, I tried to persuade the poor fellow to come back to me, while at the same time I advanced on the nearest of the savages, who was so surprised to see me, he stopped dead in his tracks.

Loath to fire, I knocked him senseless with the butt of my gun and the other one, who was some way behind him, also stopped. I could see, however, that he had a bow and arrow and was fitting it to shoot at me, so I was obviously obliged to shoot at him first. I unloaded the barrels of one gun, and killed him at the first shot.

The poor frightened savage now came nearer to me, kneeling down every ten or twelve steps to show that he knew I had saved his life. I smiled at him, and at length he came right up to me. He knelt down again, kissed the ground and then taking my foot, he set it upon his head.

I helped him to rise and gave him all the encouragement I knew how. I beckoned him to follow me, and he seemed most willing to do so. But first, he turned back and covered both savages with loose earth and leaves (the first one having died without my willing it). He did this, no doubt, to conceal their deaths from their companions. Then we proceeded to my home.

He was a handsome fellow, perfectly well made, with straight strong legs. He had a good face, gentle and friendly when he smiled, with large eyes. His hair was

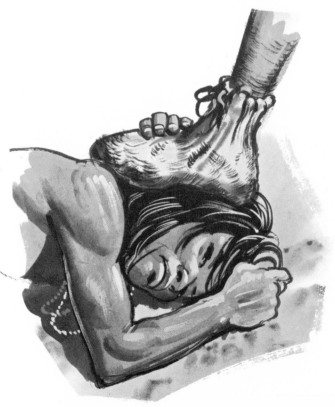

long and black, and his nose, though small, was not flat.

After he had eaten, I began to speak to him. First, I told him I would call him Friday, which was the day I had saved his life. I taught him to say Master, and Yes and No, indicating at the same time what they meant.

Next, I led him up to the top of the hill to show him that his enemies had gone. I showed him how to look through my glass so that he could see the spot where they had been. There was no sign of them and they had clearly gone, without making any search for the comrades they had left behind.

The next day, I made a little tent for him so that he would not expect to share my cave. I still felt it necessary to take a few precautions lest, his safety assured, he became aggressive himself. But I learned, in time, that no man had a more faithful, loving, and sincere servant than Friday was to me.

Friday's education

A S THE MONTHS passed I grew more and more delighted with my man Friday and I set about teaching him everything that was useful and helpful, but especially to speak and to understand me when I spoke. He was the best scholar that ever was, and was so pleased when he could understand me that we proceeded very well.

Now that there were two mouths to feed instead of one, it was clear I needed more ground to plant a larger quantity of corn to provide for both of us. Friday worked not only very willingly and hard, but did everything so cheerfully that the enterprise went ahead speedily and successfully.

He learned eagerly and well, so that my life grew much easier. I was happy, too, at finding a use for my tongue again.

One day I asked him, "Friday, how came you to be taken prisoner?"

And he answered, "They more many than my nation, in the place where me was. They take one, two, three and me."

I then asked him how far it was from our island to his country. And he told me that it was not very far, and that "a great way beyond the moon, there dwelt white bearded men." By this, I understood he was referring to the Spaniards. And, once again, my thoughts turned to leaving my desert island for ever.

After Friday came to know me much better and indeed to love me as I loved him, I told him about England, how we lived, how we worshipped God, and how we behaved to one another.

And, one day, while out walking, I said, "Friday, would you like to be in your own country again?"

"Me much glad to be at my own

nation," he answered. "You go, too."

"They will eat me if I go with you," I said. But Friday cried, "No, no, me make they no eat you. Me make they much love you."

This made up my mind for me and I told Friday that I meant to build a boat big enough to carry us both away from the island.

After a month's hard labor, we had finished our boat which was very hand-some indeed. But it cost us another two weeks to get her along, inch by inch, upon great rollers into the water. When she was floating at last, I saw she would have carried twenty men at least!

Then I began making a sail for her and with a great deal of trouble and awkward stitching for want of a needle, I eventually made an ugly three-cornered thing, which in England we called a shoulder-of-mutton sail.

The cannibals return

I WAS BUSY one morning getting together the stores for our voyage, when Friday came running back from the shore, fear all over his face.

"Master, Master!" he cried. "Yonder, one, two, three canoes!"

I comforted him as well as I could, pointing out that I was in as much danger as he was, and that the savages would certainly eat me as well as him.

Having calmed him a little I took four muskets and loaded them with two slugs and five small bullets each. I put my two pistols into my belt and I hung my great sword at my side. Then I gave Friday his hatchet and the other two guns.

"I am resolved to go down to them and kill them all," I said, "otherwise our lives will always be in danger. Are you prepared to help me?"

He nodded and said, "Me die fighting for you, Master."

With Friday close at my heels, I entered the wood and then calling to him softly, showed him a great tree. "Climb tree, Friday," I said. "Come back and tell me what you see."

He obeyed instantly and was soon back with the news that the cannibals had prisoners. One it seemed was already dead, but the other, a white-bearded man, was lying on the beach with his hands and feet bound.

I had not a moment to lose, and I ran to a high piece of ground, from where the savages were clearly in view. I took my aim at the savages, telling Friday to do the same, and together we kept up the firing until many of the wretched creatures lay dead about the fire. Some of those that remained jumped into two of the canoes and made off to sea, while the others dived into the undergrowth.

While Friday continued firing at them, I pulled out my knife and cut the poor victim's bonds, asking him in Spanish who he was.

While we talked, one of the savages that was left behind crept up behind us. The bearded man spotted him and sprang to his feet. Before I knew what was

happening he had seized one of my pistols and also my great sword, and was laying about the savage with fury.

Friday and I went down to the shore to salvage the canoe that the savages had left behind. To our surprise, we found another poor creature, lying on the bottom, bound hand and foot, and almost dead from fear and exhaustion.

To my amazement, when Friday saw him he began kissing and hugging him, crying and laughing all in the same moment. I watched, a trifle embarrassed until he recovered himself somewhat, and told me, to my great surprise, that it was his father.

Friday's joy and his concern for the old man were most moving. He fetched him water to drink and gave him raisins to eat while I attended to the Spaniard who had been further weakened by his brave attack on the savage.

Finding both men in too weak a state to walk, I made a kind of hand-barrow to lay them on, and Friday and I carried them both up to my castle.

As soon as my rescued prisoners were made comfortable, I told Friday to boil up a tasty broth. And after they had eaten, I began to talk with them. Friday's father said that he thought the escaping savages would not live out the storm, which was now blowing hard. And this put my mind somewhat at rest for I was half afraid they might return with greater numbers.

Then I turned to the Spaniard and learned that he had been shipwrecked and that only a handful of the passengers and seamen, including himself, had managed to reach the coast inhabited by the cannibals.

Together, we lived peaceably for the ensuing months, plotting and planning as to how we could both rescue the Spaniards still held prisoners by the savages, and make our escape from the island.

Finally, it was agreed that the Spaniard, now fit and strong, should take the canoe the savages had left behind. With Friday's

father to direct their course, they were to make their way to the mainland and, if possible, rescue the Spaniard's comrades.

I gave them each a musket and about eight charges of powder and ball and a plentiful supply of bread and dried grapes — enough to last them for many days.

They set sail on the day that the moon was full and, by my reckoning, in October, twenty-seven years after I had landed on my desert island. I was now full of hope that by some means or other, their voyage would bring my own rescue much nearer.

I had been waiting for them for about eight days, when a strange and unforeseen accident intervened, of which the like has not been heard of in history.

Fast asleep in my hammock, I was rudely awakened when my man Friday came running in to me, calling loudly, "Master, Master, they are come!"

I jumped up, got into my clothes and heedless of danger, ran up the hill. There, not a mile out to sea, was a boat with a shoulder-of-mutton sail, and the wind blowing pretty fair to bring her in. Farther out, and at anchor, lay an English ship.

My joy at seeing a ship, as I thought, manned by my own countrymen, was so overwhelming that I was all for running down to the shore. Holding myself in check, however, I soon saw the boat being beached. Eleven men came on shore; three of them were bound. One of the seamen carried a great cutlass and, it seemed to me, was ready to use it on the prisoners.

The seamen roared and shouted in a drunken manner and it occurred to me that they were most likely mutineers who had taken their officers prisoner. I resolved then to wait until dark, and began to prepare myself for yet another battle.

When night fell at last, Friday and I, armed to the teeth, made our way quietly shorewards. The seamen had gone off into the woods, leaving their three bound prisoners under a tree. I came as near to them as I could and then called as loud as I dared, "Who are you, gentlemen?"

They started up at the noise, but were ten times more surprised when they saw me, and the strange figure I made these days.

"He must be sent directly from heaven," said one of them at last, almost, it seemed, to himself.

"All help is from heaven," said I. "But can you put a stranger in the way to help you, for you seem in some distress?"

The poor man who had first spoken, answered, "I will tell you, sire. I was commander of that ship. My men have mutinied against me. They would have murdered me if my mate and a passenger, both of whom you see here, had not persuaded them to land us on this desert island."

It was just as I had guessed and, quickly cutting their bonds, I led them into the safety of the woods.

Then Friday and I gave muskets to all three and, acting on my instructions, the little band of us prepared to round up the seamen — none of whom were carrying firearms. This was much easier than I had anticipated for when we fell upon them, they were so surprised, they were ill-prepared to fight. No doubt my extra-ordinary appearance had something to do with their fear and subsequent willingness to surrender. The two ringleaders were shot dead by the captain which, no doubt in his eyes, was fair punishment for their wrongdoing; and the others quickly proved they were nothing but cowards at heart.

After binding our prisoners securely, I had great delight in taking the captain and his companions over my estate and he expressed the greatest admiration for everything he saw there.

Then we sat down to discuss how we might take the ship, for the captain told us she still had some twenty-seven seamen on board her.

Homeward bound

AS WE DISCUSSED what we should do, we heard the ship fire a gun as a signal for the boat to return. When their firing and their signals proved fruitless, the mutineers hoisted another boat and rowed towards the shore.

The captain, on viewing the crew through my glass, declared that at least three of the seamen were good fellows and would not fight us. But the others, he said, were desperate villains. Soon we saw seven of them come on shore, and the three who remained in the boat stood by a good distance out to wait for their comrades.

The mutineers on land now began shouting for their mates, and continued till they grew weary. Not caring it seemed to venture far from the sea, they sat down together under a tree, perhaps to consider what might have befallen the seamen and their prisoners.

At last, as night fell, it seemed they began making preparations to leave the island and signalled to their boat to come and fetch them. Seeing this, the captain grew quite desperate, thinking that once they returned to the ship, she would be lost

to him forever. Quickly, I applied my mind to thinking of a trick that might bring them back. I ordered Friday and the captain's mate to go over the creek westward, and as soon as they reached a little rising ground, to begin shouting as loud as they could.

As soon as they heard the noise, two of the men turned back and began running in the direction of the shouts. With the captain and the others, I crossed the creek out of their sight and together we surprised them before they rightly knew what was happening.

By now the boat was beached and all the seamen had come ashore. However, they were all clearly in a near state of terror on finding two more of their mates had disappeared. In their panic they split up and it was an easy matter to track them down and take them, one by one. By the time we had rounded up the last of them, they were firmly convinced that the entire island was enchanted. The captain told them that they were not his prisoners, but belonged to the commander of the island, and that he was an Englishman who might hang them all forthwith, if he so pleased.

The captain now only had to man the boats, and return to take possession of his own ship. Those of the mutineers who confessed that they had never had any liking for the enterprise, volunteered to help him in this venture.

This was more easily done than any of us had imagined, for as the boats drew aside her, the mate, with great gallantry, boarded the ship immediately and seeking out the new captain and leader, shot him dead. Upon seeing their new leader so easily killed, the rest of the seamen yielded without a fight. No sooner was the ship secured than the captain ordered seven guns to be fired to tell me of his success.

Having heard the signal, and realizing that the battle was over, I felt the extent of my exhaustion. I returned to my castle, lay down and slept very soundly till I was surprised to hear a man call me by the name of "Governor." It was the captain. Pointing to the ship, he embraced me.

"My dear friend and deliverer," he said, "there is your ship. She and all that belongs to her is yours."

I was at first ready to faint with astonishment, for at last I saw my deliverance put into my hands in the shape of a large ship ready to carry me wherever I pleased to go.

When I had recovered somewhat, we considered what was to be done with the

prisoners. And we finally agreed upon the verdict that they should be left upon the island. When I conveyed this to them, they seemed very thankful, and said they would much rather stay there than be carried to England to be hanged.

When they had declared their willingness to stay, I told them I would let them into the story of my life there. Accordingly, I recounted the whole history of the place and showed them my fortifications, the way I made my bread, planted my corn and dried my grapes. I told them the story of the Spaniards that were to be expected, for whom I left a letter, and made them promise to treat them with all fairness. Then I gave them a description of the way I managed the goats, and directions as to how to milk and fatten them and make both butter and cheese.

Having done all this, I left them the next day and, in company with the captain and his crew and my faithful man Friday, who swore he would serve me as long as I lived, I went on board the ship that was to take me to England.

I carried on board, for relics, the great goat-skin cap I had made, my umbrella and one of my parrots. Thus, I left my island on the 19th December in the year 1686, having been no less than eight and twenty years, two months and nineteen days upon it.

prisoners. And we finally agreed upon the verdict that they should be left upon the island. When I conveyed this to them, they seemed very thankful, and said they would much rather stay there than be carried to England to be hanged.

When they had declared their willingness to stay, I told them I would let them into the story of my life there. Accordingly, I recounted the whole history of the place and showed them my fortifications, the way I made my bread, planted my corn and dried my grapes. I told them the story of the Spaniards that were to be expected, for whom I left a letter, and made them promise to treat them with all fairness. Then I gave them a description of the way I managed the goats, and directions as to how to milk and fatten them and make both butter and cheese.

Having done all this, I left them the next day and, in company with the captain and his crew and my faithful man Friday, who swore he would serve me as long as I lived, I went on board the ship that was to take me to England.

I carried on board, for relics, the great goat-skin cap I had made, my umbrella and one of my parrots. Thus, I left my island on the 19th December in the year 1686, having been no less than eight and twenty years, two months and nineteen days upon it.